*S*ometimes when the wind blows hard, Great-grandma Annie tells us a story from long ago, about dust winds and tin cans and the day the angels danced in the sky.

She always begins by telling us about the land.

TIME WAS, children, when I was a young girl, I lived on a wheat farm, as flat as a breadboard.

The farm was on the Panhandle plains of Oklahoma. That's where the land reaches out straight as a handshake, like the end of a pot.

Our little house on the farm was small and brown. It had only two rooms and a lean-to kitchen for Mama, Papa, Bessie, and me.

I was the oldest and was named after Mama, because Papa said I had Mama's eyes—as big and blue as a bowl of prairie sky.

When I was twelve and Bessie was six, our sky, so big and blue, turned dark and fierce in the middle of the day. Great dust storms came blowing. They came with the drought that took hold of the land. No rain fell for a long, long time.

Mean new winds came blowing, too, scorching hot and stiff as a dragon's breath. They withered our corn. They withered our wheat. They baked our land bone-dry until it looked as cracked and old as Mama's white milk pitcher. Soon nothing grew in Papa's fields except great piles of dusty earth.

When those dust winds blew at night, dirt came right through the cracks in our little brown house. Before bed Bessie and I always stuffed the cracks with old newspaper scraps and hung wet sheets over the windows to keep the dirt from blowing in. Still it came to call like an unwanted visitor. It covered our faces with sandy grit as we slept, and in the morning our pillows would be brown, except for the spots where our heads had been.

Most mornings, too, we'd find the dust from the night lying sandy and dark across the kitchen table. After chores I liked to trace my name in the dirt as if it were a chalkboard. Sometimes I helped Bessie write out her name, pretending I was a teacher. Mama always smiled when she saw me giving lessons in the dust.

"Annie," she'd say, "you make me think nothing's so bad that it isn't good for something."

But it was hard to find anything good about the dust that took Mama. One day in the early fall she started coughing. Her coughing grew worse and worse. The doctor called it dust pneumonia. "I'll be better soon," she promised. But Mama never got better. She died just after Papa's planting, when the winter wheat lay in the ground, waiting for the snows and growing rains.

But the sky didn't cry for Mama like Bessie and I did. No rain fell. Papa held us close. "Mama is an angel now," he told us.

"Is an angel like the dust?" Bessie asked. "Going anywhere it has a mind to?"

"Just like the dust," Papa said. "Always everywhere."

With Mama gone, I kept house for Papa and Bessie. I didn't mind the hard work, but the dust made my long days even longer. On Mondays, it grayed my wash drying clean on the line. On baking days, it sifted down the walls and covered my bread rising high on the back of the cookstove. And whenever a black blizzard blew, I could barely get a meal to table for the dirt in the air.

Black blizzards rolled down from the north and smothered the sun. Bessie and I thought they looked like the end of the world coming at us.

One Sunday in April, Papa got lost in the worst black blizzard of all. He was high on the north quarter when the big roller hit. As fast as we could, Bessie and I gathered in the livestock and ran into the house to wait for Papa. We huddled around the kitchen window and watched the boiling black dirt wall blowing toward us with big chunks of earth tumbling inside it. Soon the air in the room grew thick, and we couldn't see our hands in front of our faces.

Bessie was so frightened, she held me tight and cried.

"Hush, honey," I soothed. "Papa will be home soon, and Mama's keeping watch."

"Is she still an angel?" Bessie asked me through her tears.

"A beautiful angel," I said, "dancing above the clouds."

Just then Papa stumbled in the door. He was black as Mama's frying pan and nearly choked to death from the mud-thick air. But we were never so happy to see him!

On one slow spring day, when no dust storms came blowing, I took care of Mama's garden. It was her special place—her growing quilt, she called it.

I turned over the tired earth and sowed in rows of English peas, tomatoes, cucumbers, melons, and beets. And every kind of bean—waxed, green, and butter. Then day after day I drenched the ground with heavy buckets of water I carried from the well. But the hot sun and dry winds just wilted my sweet new greens pushing up from the ground. Papa watched me sadly and shook his head. "Two hands and a bucket can't make rain, Annie," he said.

Then one morning, when I was shooing a chicken from the barn, I found a pile of old tin cans. Suddenly an idea began sprouting up in me like the seeds in my garden. My idea was a tin-can pipe—making lots of hands and buckets work together to bring water to my garden. I took the bottoms off the cans to hollow them out. Then I punched their sides through with nail holes and buried them touching end to end just under the ground.

The next day Papa ran water through my pipe from the windmill. Our windmill pulled our water up from the ground. Papa kept the windmill running all day and night. Then he rimmed around the garden with gunnysacks to keep the storms from blowing it away.

Soon my garden turned as green as a spring meadow. Papa called it a fine sight. "Pretty as Mama's growing quilt," he said.

Papa, Bessie, and I ate well from my garden all summer long. On Saturdays I raised money by selling beans and cucumbers for a dollar a bushel in town. Often I gave my vegetables away to people who couldn't pay. It just seemed like the right thing to do, life being so hard. "Your mama would be proud," folks always said to me. Papa was proud, too, he said.

In August, I canned up my vegetables in glass jars. I put a perfect seal on the top of each, just as Mama had taught me, "to keep summer safe inside."

But nothing could keep Papa's wheat and corn safe that summer from the drought and blowing winds. When his crops didn't make good, the bank wanted to take our farm. So Papa took a job with the county, leveling off the dirt drifts on the road to town. It was hot, dangerous work in the blowing storms, but with the money he earned, we were able to keep our home.

Then one terrible day, when Papa was working his road job, it felt like we *had* lost everything. Bessie called to me from the barnyard. "Come quickly, Annie, the cows are in the feed stack again!" she cried.

As I hurried from the house, a curtain near the kitchen window was drawn into the stove and caught fire on the burner. Everything was so dry the house instantly became a wall of flames. There was nothing I could do except hope it wouldn't spread. I was so sad I didn't even cry. Bessie and I just watched our little house burn to ashes before Papa came home.

Our neighbors, the Ralstons, took us in after the fire. That Sunday we all went to church together, "to take the lonesomes out of bad times," Papa said.

Then, after services, something wonderful happened. A line of cars, stretching bumper to bumper, followed us back to the Ralstons'. In the cars were all our friends and neighbors. They'd come to give us a little book with their names in it. Next to their names was the sum of money each was giving us to start again. Ten dollars from the Arthurs; five dollars from the Joneses. "Just returning a favor," they said, and pressed our hands.

My tears came easily then. I knew we'd been growing friendships in those years of dust, deep and true. Just like my garden pipe touching tin can to tin can, folks all came together to keep life going.

With the money Papa bought a pink house from Dr. Blackmer in Guymon and moved it to our land on a flatbed truck.

The first day in our new house, Bessie helped me with the baking.

"Can Mama see us in our pink house?" she asked me.

"An angel can see everything," I answered.

Then Bessie's voice began to tremble. "But, Annie, we can't see Mama anymore," she said. "You can't see an angel, even if she can see you."

Her words pulled at my heart. I knew just how she felt. It seemed the new house didn't know Mama the way our little brown house did. It felt strange and empty without her. Then suddenly, it was as if I could hear Mama talking, a whisper in the wind.

"Annie," she said, "you make me think nothing's so bad that it isn't good for something."

Lessons in the dust, I remembered.

"Maybe we *can* see an angel, Bessie," I said.

I took hold of her hand and led Bessie outside to a fence row drifted high with dirt. Carefully I turned and lay down backward in the powdery earth. Then I moved my arms and legs, slowly, back and forth, and when I stood up, I'd made in the dust a perfect angel.

I folded my arms around Bessie. We smelled all earthy and warm together from the baking and the dirt. Then we just stood there for the longest time.

We watched our angel until the sky turned dusk pink and the wind danced away with her gown in a soft prairie waltz. And all through the sky, we saw the dances of angels in the blowing dust.

Mama was near, we knew.

Sometimes when the wind blows hard, Great-grandma Annie tells us her story from long ago about the dust winds and tin cans and the angels that danced in the sky.

When she finishes, she always closes her eyes and smiles.

"Did you see them, too, children—the angels?" she asks us.

"We saw them, too, Grandma," we say.

Then we leave her alone, quiet with memories.

Author's Note

Many facts in this story—the little brown and pink houses, the tin-can garden pipe, the fire, and the friends' book of money—are true, shared with me by a wonderful woman named Annie Cronkhite Bender.

They all happened in Annie's life when she grew up near Guymon, Oklahoma—the heart of the dust storms. Between the years of 1933 and 1937, Guymon experienced 352 storms. One every five days! To Annie and the people around her, those years certainly earned their name, "the dirty thirties."

The world, however, knew Annie's land as the Dust Bowl. It received its name in 1933 from Robert Geiger, a reporter for the Associated Press. He and other journalists came to the drought-stricken five-state area of Texas, New Mexico, Colorado, Kansas, and Oklahoma to write about the severe land erosion and the catastrophic dirt storms.

They told how trains derailed from shifting dirt; how people and livestock died from dust pneumonia; and how farmland as far west as Oklahoma swept as far east as the Atlantic Ocean, stopping first to dust the desk of President Roosevelt, who was in office during those years of the Great Depression.

What could cause such giant dust storms? First there was the drought. The land needed its rains and snows to stay healthy. The farmers, too, were held to blame. Years of turning up the native buffalo grasses left the dry earth unprotected from the winds. There was nothing to hold the topsoil down, so it simply blew away.

Near the beginning of World War II, the cycle of drought was slowly replaced by rains and generous snows. The farmers learned new plowing practices as well. Instead of cutting straight furrows in the earth, their tractors now made big, sweeping arcs, like waves in the ocean, to keep the soil from blowing away. When all things worked together, the days of the Dust Bowl finally came to an end.

But Annie's story goes on, a reminder that hope is always a helping hand away, and that the worst of times can bring out the best in people.